OLIVER
AND THE
SEAWIGS

OXFORD
UNIVERSITY PRESS

Great Clarendon Street, Oxford OX2 6DP
Oxford University Press is a department of the University of Oxford.
It furthers the University's objective of excellence in research, scholarship,
and education by publishing worldwide in

Oxford New York

Auckland Cape Town Dar es Salaam Hong Kong Karachi
Kuala Lumpur Madrid Melbourne Mexico City Nairobi
New Delhi Shanghai Taipei Toronto

With offices in

Argentina Austria Brazil Chile Czech Republic France Greece
Guatemala Hungary Italy Japan Poland Portugal Singapore
South Korea Switzerland Thailand Turkey Ukraine Vietnam

Oxford is a registered trade mark of Oxford University Press
in the UK and in certain other countries

British Library Cataloguing in Publication Data

Data available

ISBN: 978-0-19-273488-4

7 9 10 8 6

Printed in Great Britain by Bell and Bain Ltd, Glasgow

Paper used in the production of this book is a natural,
recyclable product made from wood grown in sustainable forests.
The manufacturing process conforms to the environmental
regulations of the country of origin.

OLIVER
AND THE
SEAWIGS

BY PHILIP REEVE
AND SARAH McINTYRE

OXFORD
UNIVERSITY PRESS

FOR ROSE & KI
(AS I PROMISED AT YOUR WEDDING:
CONGRATULATIONS, YOU TWO!)
—SARAH

FOR MARIANNE & HOWARD
—PHILIP

ONE

Oliver Crisp was only ten years old,
but they had been a busy and exciting
ten years, because Oliver's mother
and father were explorers.

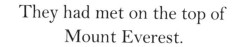

They had met on the top of
Mount Everest.

They had been married
at the Lost Temple of
Amon Hotep, and had spent
their honeymoon searching for the
elephants' graveyard. And when
young Oliver was born they simply
bought themselves a back carrier and
an off-road baby buggy and went
right on exploring.

MEH

But at last there came a day when Mr and Mrs Crisp realized there was just nothing left to explore. They had trekked to the headwaters of all the great rivers, and stood on the summits of all the unconquered mountains. Thanks to them, the Lost City of Propacopaketl was lost no longer; the Mystery of the Mokele Mbembe Marshes had been solved. There were no more blank spaces left on the map.

So they packed their belongings aboard their explorermobile and drove home to the house which they owned but had hardly ever lived in, by Deepwater Bay, near the little

seaside town of St Porrocks. 'No more exploring for us,' they told each other sadly. 'It's time we settled down.'

Oliver wasn't sad, though. He was excited. He was tired of living the explorer's life. The house he was coming home to was one he'd only seen on holidays; brief two-week breaks before fresh expeditions. Ten years on the move! No time to make friends, or feel at home anywhere. No time to go to school. He'd never even had a proper bedroom of his own, just a bunk in the back of the explorermobile, and all his things were hidden away in trunks and storage boxes in the spaces under the explorermobile's seats. He thought it would be exciting to have a whole house to live in, and wake up every day to the same view. At Deepwater Bay he would have his own bedroom and bathroom, and he would be starting next term at the school in St Porrocks. (That might not sound so good to you, but Oliver had never been to school, and he was excited about that, too.)

He perched between his parents as Mum steered the explorermobile carefully along the winding lanes. He was waiting for the moment when Deepwater Bay came in sight.

'It's not a very pretty house,' his mother reminded him. 'It's really rather old and creaky, and the wind blows right through it. It needs lots of work doing, but we never found the time. Or the money. There's not a lot of money in exploring.'

'OK,' said Oliver, but he didn't stop feeling excited.

They came over a sudden headland and there it was; the blue bay all dotted with shaggy, steep-sided islands. The house stood at the top of the beach. It was big and grey, with orange lichen dappling its roof.

'Wow!' said Oliver.

'Wow!' said his dad.

'Wow!' said his mum, stopping the explorermobile on a curve of the steep lane and just sitting there, staring in sheer amazement.

'Wow!' they all three said again. Oliver was pleased that his parents sounded just as thrilled as he was. Then he looked at them, and saw that it was not the house that they were looking at, but all those scruffy islands in the bay.

'Where have *they* come from?' asked his father. 'I don't remember *them . . .*'

Mum was rustling the map. 'They are not marked here!' she gasped.

'Nine . . . ten . . . fifteen . . .' Dad muttered. 'They must be new islands! Volcanic, probably . . .'

'Unmapped!' said Mum.

'Uncharted!' said Dad.

'Unexplored!' they whispered, both together.

Oliver sighed. He'd seen them like this before, whenever they heard of a vanished city or a forbidden tomb. Still, he thought, at least they can explore these islands from home. He looked happily at the house while Mum,

with her eyes on the islands, started
the explorermobile again and took it
screeching down the zigzag lane to
the beach.

Oliver started unpacking at once.
While his mother and father fetched
down their inflatable dinghy from the
explorermobile's roof, he unlocked the
house and carried boxes and bags and
suitcases inside. He walked through
the big, echoey, dimly familiar rooms,
whisking dust sheets off the armchairs
which had waited so long for someone
to come and sit in them again. He ran

upstairs to his room and bounced on
the bed. He loved his room already;
the way the sunlight came into it and
made a long golden stripe down the
wallpaper. He opened the window
to let in the air, and the sea wind,
and the cries of the gulls.

'Oliver!' called his
mother and father. They were down
at the sea's edge, ready to go off
and explore the new islands. They
stood in the shallows, waving.

Their inflatable dinghy tossed between them as the waves broke under it.
'Oliver! Come with us!'
'I'm busy!' Oliver shouted back. 'Why don't you go and have a look around without me? I'll be all right.'

He sighed. He knew his parents loved him. It was just that, sometimes, he had the feeling that they loved exploring more.

The little dinghy's outboard motor drowned out the seagulls with its angry-bee buzz as Mum steered through the surf. It circled a small island just off-shore, then took off with a roar across the bay towards the larger ones.

Oliver brought his suitcase upstairs and opened it. Carefully he set out his favourite things on shelves and on the windowsill. He arranged his books on the shelf beside his bed. He hung up his clothes in the cupboard. The bar of sunlight moved along the wall. And suddenly Oliver realized that it was quite a long time since he'd heard the outboard or his parents' voices.

He went to the window and leaned out. Deepwater Bay was deserted, and the evening sun shone golden on the waves. There was no sign of Mum and Dad. The islands had vanished. There was only the orange inflatable dinghy, washing back to shore upon the evening tide.

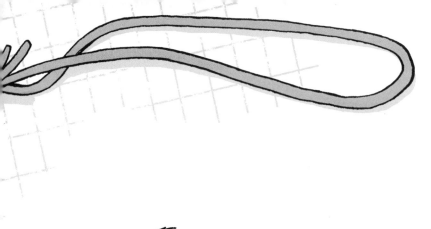

TWO

Most people would be a bit alarmed to find that their parents had disappeared along with a whole bunch of uncharted islands. They might feel inclined to phone the police, or the coastguard, or just run about shouting. Not Oliver. He was a Crisp, and made of sterner stuff than that. He hadn't panicked when his baby-buggy was carried off by an eagle on the expedition to the Forgotten Mesa.

He hadn't lost his cool when his
parents took him on that ill-advised
cycling trip around the crater of Mount
Firebelly ('But it's supposed to be an
extinct volcano!' Dad had yelled, while
lava-bombs bounced off their cycling
helmets.) He had barely batted an eyelid
when a bear stole his sleeping bag
on the north face of Mount Rainier.
He barely batted one now: just ran
downstairs and out on to the beach,
looking around in case his parents had
come ashore without him noticing.

But the beach, in the wintry afternoon
sun, was long and empty and completely
parent-free. The orange dinghy rasped
against the sand, down on the foreshore
where the small waves kept spreading
neat doilies of foam under it.

Oliver pulled it further up the beach
and wondered what to do. Then he
noticed that there was still one island
left in the bay. It was the littlest and

lowest and least interesting of them, the one his mum and dad had ignored when they went motoring off to explore the taller ones. Even from the shore, with the low sun shining in his eyes, Oliver could see that they were not on it. But perhaps it held some clue to where they'd gone . . .

He ran back to the explorermobile and packed a rucksack with Useful Things. Then he locked the house up and put a note on the front door which read

How he hoped he would be!

      He scampered to where
the dinghy waited, and shoved it out into
the sea again. *Wap, wap* went the waves,
slapping its blunt orange nose. Oliver
heaved himself aboard. He couldn't work
the outboard motor because his arms
weren't strong enough to tug the starter
cord, but there were oars stowed neatly
on the bottom-boards and he pulled them
out and started rowing. It didn't take him
long to reach the island, where he

pulled the dinghy up on the sheltered,
shoreward side.

The island was just as small as it had
looked from the beach. Clumps of greyish
grass sighed softly as the sea wind
stirred them. There were snaggles of
driftwood, festoons of weed, a length of
old tarred rope. There was a ramshackle
heap of twigs balanced on the pile
of boulders which were the highest
place on the island. That was all.
It took Oliver less than

a minute to walk right across the island to the far shore, where he stood looking out to sea. All his hopes of finding clues faded, like the foam which kept washing around his toes and melting into the wet sand.

'Mum!' he shouted. 'Dad!'

The echoes came back at him from the cliffs around the bay. Echoes, but no reply.

'Mum!' he shouted, louder still. 'Dad!'

'Oh, put a sock in it, won't you?' grumbled a creaky voice behind him. 'Some of us are trying to sleep!'

A pair of beady blue eyes were glaring at Oliver over the brim of that twig-heap on the island's crown. The heap was a nest, and the eyes belonged to the bird who owned it.

'But birds don't talk!' protested Oliver.

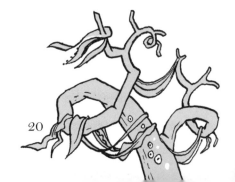

20

'Parrots do,' the bird said.

'Not really, not properly,' Oliver protested. 'And anyway, you're not a parrot.'

'Indeed I'm not,' the bird sniffed. It stood up in its nest and spread its enormous, dirty-white wings. 'I am a Wandering Albatross. *Diomedea exulans.* Though you may call me Mr Culpeper. And now you had best get back to shore, or you will be a wanderer too.'

'What does that mean?' wondered Oliver.

'Tsk,' the bird said, 'don't they teach you youngsters anything these days? Not all islands stay where you put them. Some move about. Here one minute, gone the next. This is one of them. That's why I nested on it, of course. I'm not stupid. Why go flapping about the world when I can just roost here and let the island do the wandering?'

Oliver looked down at the island. Between his feet he saw rock, sand, grit, dune-grass and ground-down seashells. It didn't look as if it were going anywhere.

'How do they move?' he asked.

'Who cares?' said Mr Culpeper, shrugging his wings.

'Where are they going?'

'Who knows? said Mr Culpeper. 'But all the others have gone already, so this one won't stay much longer.'

As he spoke, the island shuddered. Small stones spilled and rattled, trickling down.

'Hop in your boat and be off with you,' said the albatross.

'No!' said Oliver. 'Not me. I'm staying. Wherever those islands went, I must go too. My mum and dad were on one of them, you see.'

'That noisy couple?' said Mr Culpeper. 'Suit yourself, but you'd be better off without them, if you want *my* opinion.'

Oliver wasn't listening any more. The island lurched, almost throwing him off his feet. He crouched down. He curled his fingers and toes into the sand like roots, clinging on. The island sank a little. Water bubbled whitely around its edges. Then it turned slowly around and started to move out of Deepwater Bay, following the golden pathway that the evening sun had painted on the waves.

As soon as he was used to the movement, Oliver ran round to where he'd left his boat and made sure it was still safe above the tideline. Looking back, he watched the shore fall swiftly behind. A fiery shard of the sunset reflected for a moment from the window of his own bedroom, and he felt very sad that he would not be sleeping there that night. He almost launched the boat and rowed back to the beach. It was not too far, not quite, not yet . . . But there would be no point in going home without Mum and Dad. Without them, it wasn't really home at all.

So he turned his back on it, and watched

the sun dip down into the western sea, and ate a sandwich.

'What's that you're eating?' asked Mr Culpeper.

'Tuna mayonnaise,' said Oliver.

The albatross snorted. 'New-fangled muck.' He spread his wings and soared out over the ocean in the twilight, dipping down to snatch a fish out of the waves.

Oliver sat watching the empty sea, hoping for a glimpse of the other islands. He watched until it grew too dark to see anything at all, and then curled up in a grassy space among the rocks, put his rucksack under his head for a pillow, and slept.

All through the night the island kept moving. Oliver slept soundly, soothed by the island's steady motion and the snore of the sea upon its shores. Then, through his dreams, he heard another sound.

'Doof' it went. And, 'Ow!'

Oliver sprang awake. The sky was palest grey, and a few last stars were fading. A wind from the west whispered the grasses.

'Bother!' said someone nearby.

It wasn't Mr Culpeper. The albatross was sleeping still, safe in his scruffy nest with his head stuffed under his wing.

'Mum?' said Oliver hopefully. 'Dad?'

He clambered over the rocks to the beach. There on the shore sat a mermaid, rubbing her nose. 'Who put this island here?' she asked.

'Not me,' said Oliver.

He had never seen a mermaid before. In fact, he had thought they were just in stories. But then he'd never seen a moving island or a talking *Diomedea exulans* till yesterday, so he wasn't as surprised as he might have been. The mermaid seemed to be about his own age, and she was starting to get a black eye.

'There I was, swimming along, minding my own business,' she said, 'and suddenly there's an island in the way.

It's a danger to shipping, that's what
it is. It's a wonder I wasn't knocked
unconscious.'

'Have you seen any other islands?'
asked Oliver. 'My mum and dad are on
one. I'm looking for them.'

'Sorry,' said the mermaid. 'I didn't even
see this one. My eyesight isn't very
good. I can hardly see you. Come over
here; you're just a blur.'

Oliver went closer. The mermaid
frowned at him with vague, blue eyes.

'Well,' she said, 'you're an
          odd-looking character.'

Oliver thought that seemed pretty rich, coming from someone who was at least half fish, but he was a polite boy and did not try to argue. Instead he said, 'My name's Oliver.'

'Mine's Iris,' said the mermaid. 'You don't know of a place called Farsight Cove, do you? I was told there's a beach optician there. That's where I was going when your silly island got in my way.'

This was not the first time her short-sightedness had got Iris into trouble. Apart from anything else, it made other mermaids laugh at her. Well, it was *one* of the things that made them laugh. All her sisters and cousins were beautiful creatures with eyesight as clear as their singing voices, and they liked to sit on rocks with comb in one hand and mirror in the other and sing eerie songs at passing sailors. Perhaps it was because mer*men* were all rather dull, stay-at-home sorts who didn't much like mermaids' company and preferred to lounge about in their grottoes reading newspapers and discussing the latest finball results. At any rate, the mermaids enjoyed the thought of all those sailors going home and telling everyone about the lovely mermaids who had sung to them, and being haunted by their singing ever after.

Iris was nothing like that at all. She was rather plump, and she could never remember where she'd put her comb and mirror. She couldn't see the point of sitting on rocks and caterwauling all day. The one time she tried singing to a handsome fisherman in his boat it had turned out not to be a handsome fisherman or a boat at all, just a passing walrus.

'Sorry,' she told it. 'From a distance you looked just like a little brown boat with a man sitting in it.'

'Hmmm,' said the walrus. 'You need to

get your eyes tested, dear.' And it told her about the beach optician at Farsight Cove.

Oliver had heard about this beach optician too. He remembered his mum and dad talking about the dotty old man who wheeled his barrow of eyecharts, instruments and glasses down the path to the cove each day and sat there on the sand, waiting for mermaids. They had laughed and shaken their heads because they didn't believe in mermaids. Oliver looked hard at Iris and decided that there was no way he couldn't believe in her.

'Farsight Cove is quite close to Deepwater Bay . . . ' he told her. 'But they must both be miles and miles away by now. This island is moving, you see. It's been moving all night.'

'Of course it has,' said Iris. 'It's one of the Rambling Isles.'

'The *whats*?'

'The Rambling Isles. They're not really islands at all. They're alive, although they're made of stone. They wander the oceans, and they're always getting mistaken for ordinary islands, but really they're more like very big stony giants.'

'Oh,' said Oliver. 'Well, where is it going?'

'How on earth should I know?' asked Iris. 'You really do say the strangest things. I expect it's just rambling around, collecting stuff. That's what Rambling Isles *do*. But I suppose you could always ask it.'

Oliver looked around, bewildered. How could he ask rocks and stones and grass where they were going? Well, he could ask them, but how could he expect them to reply?

'Oh, I'll do it,' said Iris wearily. She slapped the nearest rock as hard as she could. 'Hello?' she shouted.

The movement of the island changed. It slowed, and turned from side to side. Mr Culpeper woke up with a squawk and demanded to know what was happening.

Slowly, the island lifted from the sea. There was a rush and gurgle of falling water draining from its edges. It rose cliff-high and the waves rolled past it far below. Oliver went to its raggedy edge and looked over.

He saw that the island was really just the top of a vast, stony head. The grass was its hair.

Water ran down its face; limpets stubbled its cheeks; seaweed and old carrier bags were tangled in its bushy eyebrows. Two big eyes peered up at Oliver.

THREE

Oliver was startled
(and Oliver was *not* a
boy who startled
easily). 'It's got a
face!' he said.

'Of course it's got a
face,' said Iris. Oliver waved at the
Rambling Isle. 'Um . . . ' he said.

'Hello,' Iris told it. 'He wants to
know where you're going.'

The Rambling Isle watched
them thoughtfully. It wasn't used
to being talked to. It was years
and years since it had spoken. It
hadn't even realized that there
was anybody on its head until

these two small upside-down faces appeared.

'Please,' said Oliver, 'I have to find those other islands. My mum and dad were on one. That's why I need to know where you're all going.'

The Rambling Isle opened its cave of a mouth. It cleared its throat with a crumbly rumble like masses of rock shearing and shifting deep in the earth. '*They* are all going to the Hallowed Shallows,' it said, 'for the Night of the Seawigs.'

Oliver was starting to feel dizzy, hanging upside down like that. He sat upright.

'What's a Seawig?' he asked.

'Haven't you heard?' said Iris. 'Every seven years the Rambling Isles all gather together at the Hallowed Shallows to show off their treasures. They love to collect things, you see; all the bits of flotsam that the sea washes up on their heads. They're very proud of their collections. On the Night of the Seawigs, each of them wears a wig made of all the treasures it has gathered on its travels. The one with the finest wig is declared the winner. It is a great honour. Everyone makes a huge fuss of them. They become Chief Island for the next seven years, and they get to order the other islands about if they want to, and choose all the best bits of wig for themselves.'

'I bet Thrumcap wins this time,' said the island. 'Or Dimsey. They always have the best seawigs. Of course, *they* have crinkly, complicated coastlines. All sorts of interesting things get stuck on *them*. Most of what washes up on my shores washes straight off again. Look at me! All I have to show for my wanderings are a few bits of old rope and a stupid bird's nest.'

Oliver tried to think of something encouraging he could say that would cheer up the poor island, but it was true: its wig was a mess. Its summit was mostly bald rock, with those tussocks of grassy hair sprouting here and there, and rather a lot of albatross poo, now that Oliver came to look critically at it.

'Who are you talking to?' asked Mr Culpeper, stalking importantly down the beach. 'And whose nest is he calling stupid?'

'I don't even know whether I can be bothered making the journey,' the island went on, in its deep and mournful voice. 'You can't imagine the wonderful seawigs which will be on display at the Hallowed Shallows. And there I'll be, with my bit of rope and my bird's nest. The others will all laugh at me. Perhaps I'll just give it a miss this time.'

'No!' said Oliver. He hung over the beach edge again. 'You must go! Or at least tell me how to get there, so I can find Mum and Dad!'

'Oh, it's not a place you could get to,' said Iris airily. 'Not on your own.' She hung upside down beside him with her wet hair dangling. 'The Hallowed Shallows aren't that sort of place at all. They are the place where all the old things of the sea went to live once people in your world stopped believing in them. Actually they are where I live too, only I came out to find that optician, and I couldn't, and now I can't find my way home either.' She blinked short-sightedly. Oliver thought he saw tears beginning to gather in her eyes.

He fetched the oily length of nylon rope he'd noticed on the tideline yesterday. He tied one end firmly round a rock, then lowered himself down in front of the island's face.

'Did you hear that?' he said. 'We both need to go to the Hallowed Shallows. Please say you'll take us there.'

'Oh, I don't know . . . ' said the island, glumly.

Oliver frowned, swaying in front of those huge eyes like a hypnotist's watch. 'Look, do you have a name?'

he asked.

'Me?' said the island, dolefully. 'A name? No. Some of the bigger Rambling Isles have been mistaken for real islands by sailors and explorers, who gave them the most splendid names, but no one ever noticed me.'

'Not at all?' said Iris.

'Well, someone put a sign up on me once, when I went to sleep for a few years near the mouth of a river.

But it fell off. Anyway, I can't go around calling myself "Danger: Submerged Rocks", can I?'

'Well, you need a name,' said Oliver, looking up at those craggy features, at the clinging barnacles and clumps of weed. 'I'm going to call you . . . Cliff.'

'Cliff . . . ' said the island, trying it out. He sounded pleased. '*Cliff . . .* '

'Now listen, Cliff,' said Oliver. 'How long is it till this Seawigs contest?'

'We gather at the Shallows tomorrow night,' said Cliff.

Iris nodded. 'That's right. All my mermaid friends are going. They're going to perch on rocks and sing; it's completely lame.'

'Well then, Cliff,' said Oliver, 'you've got all of today and tomorrow to gather some really brilliant things to decorate your seawig. We'll help!'

'Will you?' sniffed the poor island, looking hopefully at him.

'Will we?' asked Iris.

'Course we will,' said Oliver. 'Let's think. What would be the best things you could possibly have on your wig? You've already got me, and Iris, and the inflatable dinghy . . . '

'He's got an albatross, too,' said Iris. 'It can stand on the top and spread its wings or something.'

'Excuse me,' said Mr Culpeper, coming to peer over the edge beside her. 'I am *Diomedea exulans*, I am, and a particularly fine specimen, too. I am not some funfair attraction! "Spread its wings", indeed.' He sniffed loudly. 'It seems to me that this island has gone to the dogs. It used to be such a nice, quiet place. Now I can hardly move for boys and mermaids. I don't like the sound of this Seawigs affair at all. It sounds like a lot of noise and bother to me.'

'Don't listen to him,' Oliver told the island. 'Just think! What are the most wonderful things that an island could wear?'

'Well, there's always shipwrecks,' said Cliff. 'Shipwrecks are very stylish.'

'The dinghy is a sort of wreck,' Oliver pointed out.

'It's just stranded,' said Cliff sadly. 'That's not the same thing at all.'

'He's right,' said Iris dreamily, draping her tail in a rock pool. 'What he needs is a really spectacular wreck. What about the *Water Mole*?'

Oliver frowned. 'I've heard of that. It was the world's first submarine. The king of Spain built it to ferry treasure from his gold mines without English pirates noticing, but it didn't work too well. It sank, and nobody knows where.'

Iris coughed, and pointed modestly to herself.

'You mean, you know where we could

find it?' Oliver asked.

'I ran into it while I was swimming around,' Iris said, rubbing thoughtfully at a fading bruise upon her elbow. 'It's on an undersea mountain not far from here.'

'Ooh, a submarine?' said Cliff, sounding hopeful for the first time. 'I don't think any of the other islands has a submarine!'

'Well, let's go and find the *Water Mole* then,' said Oliver, 'and then hurry to the Hallowed Shallows and see what those other isles think of it! I bet they'll declare you the winner in an instant!'

Cliff nodded happily, almost tumbling his two passengers off into the sea. He'd never really thought of himself as a winner of anything before, but Oliver spoke with such certainty that he could almost hear the voices of his fellow Rambling Isles as they cheered his wonderful wig. He sank back down into the waves until the top of his stony head became an island once again, and with Iris shouting directions he set off, surging through the water with a steady, confident motion.

Oliver lay on the edge of the beach

and looked down through the water. He could dimly see Cliff's huge, rocky limbs moving far beneath him in the depths. How strange to think there were such things as Rambling Isles in the world, and he had never even heard of them!

FOUR

After Cliff had been striding along for
an hour or two, Oliver saw a shape
on the sea ahead. Then another. They
looked like small, stony islands, but he
couldn't be certain of that any more. He
pointed the islands out to Iris. 'Are they
more Rambling Isles?'

The mermaid peered in the direction he
was pointing. 'I think they were once,'
she said. 'But they've settled down.'

'What does that mean?'

'It means just what it sounds like.

Some of them lose the urge to keep wandering. They give up collecting bits and pieces for their seawigs. And once they stop moving they sort of take root; silt and sand pile up around their feet, and weed grows on them, and coral, and there they stay.'

One of the settled islands was quite close now. Looking down through the waves, Oliver thought he could see its stony face, blurred by weed and masked with barnacles.

'Are they dead?' he asked. 'Or just asleep?'

'They're settled,' said Iris. 'They are just islands now.'

'I hope Cliff never settles,' said Oliver. 'I like him rambling about. I wouldn't want him to be just an island.'

'Oh, don't worry,' said Iris, and swished her tail in the rock pool, cleaning the sand from between her scales. 'Once he has the *Water Mole* on top of him he'll win for sure. It's completely brilliant.'

Oliver nodded, hoping she was right. Then a bad thought struck him. 'Iris? How can you find your way back to this submarine wreck if you can't even find your own way home?'

'I can smell it, silly,' said Iris. 'It's in a very smelly patch of sea. Can't *you* smell it yet?'

Oliver sniffed. Sure enough there was a scent on the air of green things growing and rotting.

Hour after hour the scent grew stronger, and that afternoon they saw a darkness that lay like a green shadow on the sea ahead. Soon it stretched from horizon to horizon. As they entered its outer fringes Oliver realized that the whole face of the ocean was clogged with drifting weed.

'We must be in the Sargasso Sea!' he said excitedly. 'Sailors fear it because their ships get becalmed here, and the weed tangles round them and traps them.'

'No, this is a completely different place,' said Iris. 'It's called the Sarcastic Sea, and sailors fear it because the weed keeps making horrid, hurtful comments about them.'

Sure enough, as Cliff carried them deeper into the weed, they began to hear its little mocking voices calling out to them.

'Oh, a *mermaid*! That's *just* what we need!' and 'Nice seawig, mate!' and 'I love the inflatable dinghy . . . Orange is such a *tasteful* colour.' And you could tell that it didn't mean any of the things it said, in fact it meant exactly the opposite, and all its comments were followed by scornful sniggers, or whispery conversations that ended in laughter. The weed of the Sarcastic Sea was very sarcastic weed indeed.

As Cliff ploughed onwards

great clumps of the stuff began piling
up on the beach, and Oliver noticed that
as well as the little bladders that helped
to keep ordinary types of seaweed afloat
its strands were dotted with beady eyes,
which all looked witheringly at him.
He took out his notebook and made a
sketch, knowing that his mum and dad
would be interested when he found
them.

But the weeds did not much like being snagged on Cliff's beaches, because once they were out of the waves Mr Culpeper stalked around pecking at the tiny crabs and water bugs which lived amongst them.

Oi! they squeaked.

Watch it with the beak!

OW!

Oliver felt sorry for the weed, and he and Iris began making their way around Cliff's shores, shovelling it back into the waves and getting precious little thanks. The floating weed soon learned to keep out of the way of the oncoming island. It drew back to make a path for Cliff, and by the time Iris told him to stop, there was a broad patch of clear water all around him.

'This is the place,' the mermaid said.

'Are you sure?' asked Oliver. This bit of the Sarcastic Sea looked just the same as all the rest to him.

'Two currents meet here,' replied Iris primly. 'The sea smells different. The *Water Mole* is right beneath us. Come and see for yourself, if you don't believe me.'

So Oliver fetched his swimming things and goggles, took a deep breath, and plunged after Iris into the waves, where a few small, left-behind strands of

seaweed still floated, sneering,
'Those swimmers really suit
you (I *don't* think) . . .'

With a flick of her tail Iris
went racing down into the
green shadows. She was a
clumsy thing on dry land, but
in the water she was lithe
and nimble.

Oliver struggled after her, down past Cliff's huge, watchful face till, far below, he started to make out the summits of drowned mountains rising dimly from the ocean deeps.

By the time he saw them, the breath that Oliver had taken before he dived had almost run out. His eyes bulged and his heart hammered. Bubbles seeped from the corners of his mouth and swam towards the surface like silver jellyfish. Then, in the last instant before he had to follow them, he glimpsed the wreck. The *Water Mole* lay on the rocky top of one of those mountains. Weed and coral had transformed its hull into a strange underwater cathedral. Fish darted in and out of the shattered windows at the stern, and an eel as stripy as a gypsy's stocking had tied itself like a bow around the figurehead.

Iris bumped into the cabin, groped her way up a ladder, and perched on the top, beaming up at Oliver as if to say, 'I told you so!' But Oliver could stay no longer in her underwater world. He kicked his legs and shot back to the surface in a rush of bubbles, bursting out into the sunshine and taking deep gulps of fresh, delicious air.

Cliff rose out of the sea beside him, with falls of white water cascading off his brow.

'It's there!' said Oliver, treading water in front of the island's nose. 'It's lovely! It will make an *awesome* wig!'

But how were they to lift it? Raising wrecks was difficult, Oliver knew that. He'd seen Cliff's clumsy, stony hands. He was afraid they'd crush the *Water Mole* to splinters if Cliff simply tried to pick it up.

'You must go down to it,' he said.

'Go under the sea?' said Cliff, eyes widening. 'But what about my sands? My shells? My bits of rope? They'll all wash off if I go under!'

'And more to the point, what about *my* nest?' demanded Mr Culpeper, circling above Oliver's head.

'I know!' said Oliver. He scrambled back up onto Cliff's beach and quickly gathered anything that looked as if it might float away, including the albatross's nest. He dumped it all into the dinghy and then climbed in with it.

Then, while Iris swam about below directing things (she wasn't much help because her eyesight was even worse under water than it was above, but she liked to feel important) Cliff knelt down on his gigantic underwater knees and let the waves of the Sarcastic Sea swirl over his head. Oliver put on his goggles again and hung over the edge of his dinghy with his face in the sea as the waters lifted it. Down in the green gloom far below he saw Cliff carefully edge his way towards the wreck, and glimpsed the

flash of Iris's rainbow tail as she circled, gesturing at Cliff to move left a bit, right a bit, stop, come forward . . . (She didn't realize that she had her back to Cliff. She was actually gesturing at a confused-looking whale which just happened to be passing.)

Cliff went right up to the wreck. He nudged it with his head and tugged at it with his stumpy, stony arms. At last it shifted and rolled gently sideways. Oliver jumped up. 'That's it!' he hooted, although Oliver knew the Rambling Isle couldn't hear him. 'You've done it! Now come up!'

Cliff settled the weight of the ancient submarine on his head and began to rise, carefully, carefully, with swirls of sand glittering in the sea around him. He came up under the dinghy in a great roaring and rushing and bubbling of water and a flopping and floundering of stranded fishes. Most of them were washed back into the sea as Cliff continued to rise and the waters poured off him. Soon there was beach beneath Oliver's dinghy again. On the top of Cliff's head lay the *Water Mole*, all wet and startling and shiny in the sunlight. The striped eel had slithered off and the gilded bowsprit glimmered faintly, pointing at the sky.

It was the finest wig an island ever wore.

'Yay!' shouted Oliver, jumping out of the dinghy and doing a victory dance among the rock pools.

'Yay!' said Iris, flopping ashore and wringing out her hair.

'Yay!' rumbled Cliff, and 'Yay!' cawed Mr Culpeper. Only the sarcastic strands of floating weed were unimpressed. 'Showy,' they complained, still keeping a safe distance from Cliff's shores. 'Shipwrecks are *so* last season.' But they were only seaweed, so who cared what

they thought?

Then Mr Culpeper, gliding down to perch on the coral-encrusted flagstaff, said suddenly, 'What's that?'

Oliver turned to look. There behind him on the weedy sea, an island stood. He could not believe that he hadn't noticed it before.

FIVE

It was not really an island, of course.
It was another Rambling Isle, and it
had crept out of a nearby fog bank and
sneaked up behind Cliff while everyone
was distracted by the raising of the
submarine.

Although Oliver did not recognize it, it
was one of the same islands which had
been resting in Deepwater Bay the day
his parents disappeared. He had not been
able to see it from his bedroom window

because the headland hid it, but Mr and Mrs Crisp had seen it as they motored away from the beach in their dinghy, and had steered straight towards it, because they could tell at once that it was easily the most interesting.

It was tall and rocky, and on its summit dark trees clustered. Among the trees stood a ruined temple, crumbly and overgrown. Around the temple towered huge stone heads with empty eyes and open mouths. They looked a bit like the famous statues on Easter Island. (In fact they were where the Easter islanders had got the idea from, for this Rambling Isle had passed close to Easter Island, long ago.)

'Remarkable!' Oliver's dad had shouted, as the dinghy bounced across the waves of Deepwater Bay. 'Polynesian? Pre-Columbian?'

'A whole unknown civilization!' declared Oliver's mum, snapping photos of those weird stone heads as the dinghy swept into the island's shadow and circled it, searching for a place to land.

There was a beach on the seaward side. A beach of black sand, with steps carved in the cliff behind it, winding up past crumbled walls and watchful statues to those intriguing ruins on the summit.

Poor foolish Crisps! They were so eager to explore that they did not bother dragging their dinghy up above the tideline, which everyone knows is one of the first rules of exploring. They just left it there upon the shining sand and ran up those stairs. The clicking of their cameras echoed among the ruins, and so did their excited cries, until they reached the ruined temple.

It was not quite as ruined as it had looked from sea-level. Someone had put double glazing in its windows, and a chimney poked from the roof, puffing out little curlicues of woodsmoke.

'Oh! This island is inhabited!' said Oliver's dad, trying not to sound too disappointed, even though he had hoped to be the first person to discover a lost civilization.

'But inhabited by whom?' asked his wife, imagining lost tribes, priest-kings, and ancient wisdom.

That was when the island shivered. That was when it shook. 'Earthquake!' cried Mrs Crisp, and 'Volcano!' yelled her husband. The island sank a little. Down on its shore, waves swirled up the beach, lifted the abandoned dinghy, and carried it gently out into the bay. And from the open mouths of all those stone heads there came a noise: a rustling, a whispering, a scrabbling, a jostling, a strange, demented jabbering that grew louder and louder as the island started moving out to sea . . .

And now here it stood, a few hundred yards from Cliff, with Oliver staring at it in surprise.

'Look at all those creepy old heads!' said Iris.

Cliff turned beneath them, looking. 'Oh dear!' he rumbled. 'Oh no! It's the Thurlstone!'

'What's the Thurlstone?' asked Oliver.

'It is very old, and very bad,' Cliff said. 'Bad men did human sacrifices in that temple on its top long ago, and the blood trickled down inside it and turned it wicked. They say it's quite hollow, and rotten to the core. Oh dear!'

The Thurlstone lifted itself a little way out of the water. Massive weedy shoulders rose into the sunlight. Water drained out through cracks and fissures in the isle's sides. Its mean black eyes stared hard at Cliff through veils of falling water. A mouth like a sea-cave opened and a stony voice said, 'Nice

shipwreck you have there.'

'It's ours!' Iris shouted back. 'We found it!'

Her voice sounded very small and thin and shrill after the thunder of the Thurlstone's. It boomed again. 'Don't like the mermaid, though,' it said. 'Mermaids are vulgar.'

Now that he came to look properly at it, Oliver saw that the Thurlstone was wearing quite an elaborate seawig. Loads of plaited seaweed were arranged around

74

its cliffs, glittering with bits of broken glass and shiny metal. Old flip-flops dangled from the branches of those dark and twisted trees, and among the rocks where the temple stood a trawler and a rusty battleship were perched. From the cliffs on either side of its face two big glass globes dangled in cradles of knotted rope, like earrings, or baubles on a Christmas tree. Inside the globes, something moved.

Oliver snatched his rucksack and ferreted inside it for his binoculars. He focused on one of those glassy danglers. The thing inside it was his mum. He yelped, and swung the binoculars. There inside the other globe was Dad.

The explorers seemed quite unharmed. Oliver began to jump up and down on the beach. He waved and shouted. When he looked through the binoculars again he saw that his mum had spotted him. He saw his dad scribble something in his

explorer's
notebook and press
it flat against the
inside of his
glass
prison
for
Oliver
to read:

Now his mother was
scribbling too, and
pressing a note of
her own to the glass:
  But the Thurlstone
was coming closer.
Ignoring mean comments
and backhanded compliments from the
floating weed, it shouldered its way
through the sea.

Octopuses writhed their tentacles among its eyebrows, and a shark fell out of its nose like a fierce bogey. Up on its forehead a little platform had been built, and there a boy stood, looking down.

The Thurlstone was so close by then that Oliver didn't need his binoculars any more. He could see the boy quite clearly without them. He was older than Oliver: a tall teenager, balancing precariously on beansprout legs and about to tumble clumsily into adulthood. He wore sea-boots and a sailor's uniform with all sorts of gold braid and medals and fancy finery all over it.

When the gap of open water between Cliff and the Thurlstone had narrowed to a stone's throw the Thurlstone stopped in a swirl of foam and spoke again. 'Want it,' it said, staring at the *Water Mole.*

Up on its brow the boy picked up a big brass megaphone and bellowed through it.

MY ISLAND WANTS THAT WRECK OF YOURS. YOU'D BETTER HAND IT OVER.

'Ooh, of all the cheek!' squealed Iris. 'We found it! It's ours!'

'You're not having my wig!' rumbled Cliff.

Oliver just cupped his hands around his mouth and shouted, 'Give me back my mum and dad!'

The other boy threw back his head and laughed. It was the sort of laugh that told you instantly he was not about to let poor Mr and Mrs Crisp go. 'Ha ha ha!' he cackled. 'So they are yours are they? Well, you should have taken better care of them. They make nice additions to the Thurlstone's seawig, don't you think? But not as nice as that fine submarine your island's found. Hand it over, now, and spare yourself a lot of unpleasantness.'

'Who are you, anyway?' asked Iris. 'You're very full of yourself.'

'My name,' the boy said importantly, 'is Stacey de Lacey.'

'But that's a girl's name!' blurted Oliver.

Stacey de Lacey's face turned a dark shade of red. 'Silence!' he shouted. 'Stacey is one of those names that can be for a boy or a girl! Like Hilary, or Leslie, or . . . um . . . Anyway, when the Night of the Seawigs rolls around, my Thurlstone shall have the finest wig of all! That submarine is just the thing we need to top it off, and if you won't give it to us, we shall just have to take it!'

'Mad,' said Iris in an undertone, 'quite mad.'

Stacey de Lacey clapped his hands. 'Come, my lovelies!' he shouted, and laughed with wicked glee.

From the giant statues which grinned and gurned upon the Thurlstone's head

there came a rustling, a whispering,
a scrabbling, a jostling, a strange,
demented jabbering . . .

No wonder Stacey de Lacey sounded
gleeful. It was quite a new feeling for
him, giving orders. When he'd been
growing up, nobody had ever taken much
notice of him. His parents, who were rich
and busy, barely paid him any attention.
The other children at school all hated
him. And why did they hate him? Well,
actually it was because he was a nasty,
boastful bully, but Stacey didn't realize
that: he was sure it was just because of
his name. 'Stacey can be a boy's name
too,' he would tell them, when they
laughed at it. They never believed him.
Angry and all alone, he took long walks
on the beach near his house, dreaming
of the terrible revenge he would take on
them all when he was older.

All sorts of things washed up on that beach. As Stacey de Lacey strode along with his hands in his pockets he was forever kicking aside old flip-flops, fisherman's floats, and plastic bottles with mysterious foreign labels. One day, after a storm, he found the shingle covered with stinking seaweed, uprooted from some deep hollow of the seabed. It was a type of seaweed that he had never noticed before. It had thick stalks, each as tall as Stacey, with a fat green bulb at the top. Stacey picked up one of the stalks and began cracking it like a bull whip as he stomped along. He imagined lashing his classmates with it.

'Stacey is *not* a girl's name!' he shouted. *Crack!* 'You'll be sorry when I'm famous and powerful!' he yelled. *Crack!* 'Just you wait!' he hollered. 'One day I'll . . .'

Crack, squelch, splat!

The green bulb at the end of the sea-whip burst and out came a splurt of dirty water, and something else; something that *moved*, scrabbling and burrowing its way down into the tangles of dead weed that were heaped along the tideline.

Stacey went closer and prodded the weed-piles with his toe. Something was definitely rustling around in there. He bent down for a closer look. Suddenly the weed was torn aside and a hideous little fanged and grinning face stared up at him. Then two little web-fingered hands seized the toe of his sneaker and the creature sank its teeth into the rubber.

'Yow!' shouted Stacey de Lacey, doing a triple backwards somersault in his surprise. The creature flew off his shoe. By the time he had clambered up and dusted the sand out of his eyes it was crouching on a nearby rock, watching him. It looked like an ugly little monkey with webbed hands and feet and greasy green fur.

'Get lost!' he yelled angrily.

The sea monkey cowered, and crept away over the top of the rock, out of sight.

Stacey was impressed. He wasn't used to people doing what he told them.

'Come back!' he shouted.

The monkey reappeared.

'My name is Stacey de Lacey,' he said, and watched the monkey suspiciously. It didn't laugh, it didn't even giggle.

'Stacey is not a girl's name!' he said. Still nothing. Feeling encouraged, he told it, 'You're mine! You will do everything I say!'

The monkey drew itself to attention, and saluted.

If Stacey de Lacey had been a different sort of boy he might have thought, 'I've found a friend!' But Stacey had never really wanted friends: he thought, 'I've found a servant!'

He looked around.
All about him, the beach
was littered

with whips of the
strange weed,
each with its
sea-green bulb. Was there
a monkey in every one? There must be
loads of them! Hundreds! He picked up
a strand and

squeezed the bulb till it
popped like a spot.
Out tumbled another monkey.
Excitedly, he popped another,

and then
another.
'Help me!' he ordered
the chittering,
jittering monkeys,
and they ran
with him

along the tideline,
squeezing and popping,
squeezing and popping,
until a whole army of
sea monkeys was
scuttling behind him.

Stacey de Lacey knew that his parents would never let him keep anything as stinky and repulsive-looking as these monkeys. Luckily, there was a particularly large and slimy rock pool that he knew of, around the curve of the cliffs, where nobody but he ever went. He led the monkeys there and watched them pour into the pool. They were as happy under water as above it. They crouched in the shadows of the pool and looked up at Stacey with wicked, wary eyes.

'I am your master!' he said proudly.

After that, Stacey de Lacey turned his thoughts to the sea. If sea monkeys were real, then what other strange things might the oceans hold? Between trips to the rock pool, where he fed and gloated over his growing monkey-band,

he talked to sailors at the harbour. He peered at old books in secret libraries. He learned of the Hallowed Shallows. He learned of mermaids, and drowned cities. He learned of the Rambling Isles, and of the gathering that they held on the Night of the Seawigs.

'Monkeys are all very well,' said Stacey de Lacey to himself, 'but if I had my own Rambling Isle, think how powerful I'd be then!' He liked the idea of roving the world on his own island, being mean to people.

So he started scouring the beach for interesting things the sea washed up, and leaving them above the tideline on a tall rock just off-shore. If the Night of the Seawigs was real, he thought, no Rambling Isle would be able to resist such top-notch wig ingredients. And sure enough, one foggy evening, he

heard great sloshing footsteps move through the waves towards that rock, and saw a giant shape moving in the mist. He heard the Rambling Isle grumbling to itself as it sifted through the pile of driftwood and old fishing nets he'd left. 'This stuff's no good,' he heard it say. 'This won't help me win . . . '

'Hey, Island!' shouted Stacey de Lacey. The grumbling stopped. The thing in the fog stood listening. 'You want to win this stupid Seawigs thing?' yelled Stacey. 'You should steal the best stuff from other islands' wigs. And if you can't do that, just nobble them: ruin their wigs so they can't win!'

As luck would have it, the island Stacey was talking to was none other than the bad old Thurlstone, meanest of all the Rambling Isles. The Thurlstone liked the way this boy thought. 'How?' it asked.

'With my help!' said Stacey, and as the Thurlstone loomed out of the fog to

peer down at him he spread his arms
out proudly to show it the gibbering,
jabbering swarm of monkeys
crowded on the shingle behind him.

   'I have an army of monkeys!' he
said.

That's what the green tide was,
pouring out of the mouths and
eyes of the Thurlstone's old stone
heads and rushing across the sea.
Sea monkeys! Small and smelly
in their coats of greasy green fur,
they giggled horribly as they swam
towards Cliff, or scampered across
the mats of drifting weed. 'Don't
mind us,' grumbled the weed-mats,
but the sea monkeys were immune
to sarcasm.

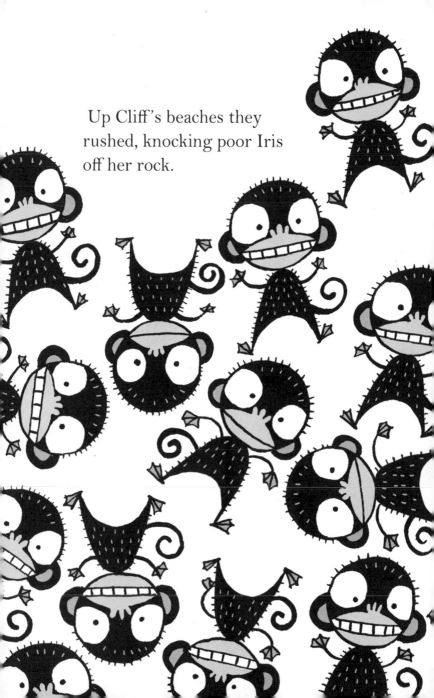

Up Cliff's beaches they rushed, knocking poor Iris off her rock.

They sank their teeth and claws into the orange inflatable and popped it, just for laughs. Oliver tried to stop them. He picked up monkeys and hurled them back at the sea, but more were landing all the time and they were scary and dangerous-looking. They bared their dirty yellow fangs and screeched at him.

The monkey tide sloshed up onto Cliff's bouldery summit and lapped around the *Water Mole*. The sea monkeys were so small that Oliver did not think they could shift the submarine, but there were so many of them that they did. The *Water Mole* lifted from its perch, afloat again on a sea of snot-green fur. Oliver and Iris had to jump out of the way as the chattering monkeys rushed back with it into the sea. The Thurlstone dipped down, till only Stacey's balcony and the old stones and the trees around the temple showed, and the monkeys swam and swirled and struggled and shoved the *Water Mole* onto his head.

'So long, losers!' called Stacey de Lacey, waving. 'We'll see you at the Hallowed Shallows—if you still think it's worth turning up, of course.'

The Thurlstone turned and moved off. The glass orbs which were Oliver's parents' prisons bobbed on either side of it, towed on their tethers of rope, with Mr and Mrs Crisp waving sad goodbyes inside them. Sea monkeys went scurrying back to their nests in the old stone heads. The *Water Mole* shone so brightly in the slanting sunlight that Oliver could see the gleam of it long after the wicked island had dwindled to a speck on the horizon.

That went well! said the watching weed.

SIX

As the Thurlstone vanished, all Cliff's
new-found hopefulness drained away.
The fight went out of him. Iris and
Oliver felt him slump. They couldn't
blame him. Poor old giant! So much of
his golden sand and drifts of flotsam had
been washed away
when he stooped to
fetch the *Water Mole*.
Now it was gone, his
stony head was even more
bare than before.

'Now what shall we do?' asked Iris.

'Go after that Thurlstone, of course!' shouted Oliver. 'Quick, Cliff! Follow him!'

Cliff lifted his cave mouth out of the waves to say, 'What's the point? He's beaten me.' Then he subsided again.

'You can't just let him win!' said Oliver. 'Is he the sort of island who deserves to win the Night of the Seawigs? And as for that Stacey de Lacey . . . ! Go after them, and get the *Water Mole* back!'

'How?' rumbled Cliff. 'They have an army of monkeys.'

'He's got a point,' said Iris.

'Then go to the Hallowed Shallows!' insisted Oliver. 'Tell everyone what Stacey and his Thurlstone did . . . '

'They won't listen to me,' said Cliff wearily. 'They'll be too busy admiring the Thurlstone's marvellous seawig, and laughing at me.'

'So what are you doing to do?' Iris asked.

Cliff sighed. 'I'm going to settle,' he decided.

'No!' yelled Oliver.

'I should have done it years ago,' Cliff went on. 'What's the point of all this tramping around, collecting stuff? I'm going to stand here and grow roots and forget I ever was a rambler. I'll become just an island. That's all I'm good for. I'm useless. Finished. Washed up.'

He sank back slowly into the sea. 'No!' shouted Oliver again. He did a dance of frustration, shin-deep in the wavelets which washed Cliff's shores. But no amount of stamping or shouting would make Cliff come up again. Oliver remembered the sad, lifeless, settled isles which Iris had shown him on the way to the Sarcastic Sea. He imagined the sand and silt slowly piling up around Cliff's feet.

'Oh dear,' said Iris, with salt tears dripping off her chin. 'I think he means it.'

'*Now* look what you've done,' sniffed Mr Culpeper, fussily rearranging his nest, which had been terribly knocked about by those swarming sea monkeys. 'If you hadn't dragged us here in search of that stupid wreck this would never have happened. It's all your fault.'

'Well I'm not going to let Stacey de Lacey win,' said Oliver. Years of exploring had taught him that you don't solve problems by sitting around complaining about them. You have to *do* something. That's how his mum and dad had saved him from that Komodo dragon. That's how they'd escaped from the dungeons of M'bumbi M'bumbi. He struck an explorer-ish pose on the shore and said, 'I'm going to go after that Thurlstone and show it that it can't just go around snitching other people's shipwrecks and kidnapping mums and dads!'

'That's all very well and good,' said

Iris, 'but ARMY OF MONKEYS, remember? Oh, and your boat's gone all flop.'

Oliver ignored the reminder about the monkeys. He hadn't yet thought of any way that he could deal with them. He had an answer to the part about the boat, though. He opened his explorer's pack and triumphantly pulled out a foot pump and a Punctured Dinghy Repair Kit. One hour of patching and pumping later, he was ready. He shoved the dinghy into the waves and hoisted himself aboard. He tugged the motor's starter cord.

It didn't work. It never did. You needed big muscly arms like Dad's to make it start.

Iris looked on doubtfully. 'I suppose I could help,' she said.

'Oh yes, you'll be a lot of use!' snapped Oliver, so sarcastically that even the seaweed was shocked. 'Your arms are even feebler than mine!'

'Oh, I don't mean like that,' sniffed the mermaid. She unhooked the motor from the stern of the dinghy and dropped it on the shore. Then, before Oliver could ask how that was supposed to help, she scrambled half aboard the dinghy, with her tail hanging off behind.

'Shove off!' she said.

'Ooh, isn't she *rude*!' whispered the weed, admiringly.

'I mean shove the *dinghy* off.'

Oliver shoved. As the dinghy drifted into deeper water Iris started to flap her tail up and down, driving them away from the shore.

It was difficult to steer at first, but they soon worked it out. Iris took the dinghy on a farewell circuit of the island. Oliver looked over the side, down through the waves at the great, dim cliff face of Cliff's face looming there. He couldn't see if Cliff's eyes were open or closed. He couldn't tell if the Rambling Isle was watching his friends leave, or just too sad to care. He waved anyway.

Mr Culpeper flapped over to perch on the dinghy's prow. 'I might as well come with you,' he said. 'After all, you'll need help finding that thieving island, I suppose.'

So the albatross took off again, soaring towards the horizon, and the mermaid-powered dinghy followed him, splashing along the lane of open water which the Thurlstone had left through the sarcastic weed.

It was tiring work for poor Iris. Every few minutes she had to stop and rest while Oliver refuelled her by feeding her caramel bars from his lunch box. But at last the Sarcastic Sea was left behind.

'I wonder why Stacey de Lacey is so keen to help the Thurlstone win the contest, anyway?' wondered Oliver. But Iris was too busy being an outboard motor to reply.

Mr Culpeper flew above them, calling down directions. At first there was no need, for Oliver and Iris could see the Thurlstone, far ahead. But as the day wore on the thieving isle drew away from them, and a strange haze arose. Soon it was hard for even the sharp-eyed albatross to see very far. 'We are coming near to the Hallowed Shallows,' said Iris.

They began to pass other Rambling Isles. At first they looked like normal islands, but they were all moving, and all in the same direction, with white wakes of foam stretching behind them. Some were as small and tatty as Cliff. Some were magnificent. There was one who had sculpted a sort of volcano on his upper parts, and lit a fire in it so trails of smoke rings mingled with the haze. There was one who had drizzled wet sand onto her head to build up teetering pinnacles and spires, and another who had arranged miles and miles of weed into a massive beehive, with a small ship stuck in the middle of it. None of them paid the slightest attention to the dinghy.

'If only Cliff was here!' said Oliver, feeling sad that they had left their own Rambling Isle behind.

'The rest would only laugh at him,' said Iris. 'Some of those seawigs are to die for!'

Meanwhile, back in the Sarcastic Sea, Cliff was thinking sadly of his friends. He had never had actual *people* living on him before, and he missed them now that they were gone. Not only that, the seaweed had drifted closer now that he was not moving, and it kept jeering and sniggering at him and saying how *brave* it thought he was.

'No,' he told himself. 'It's no use worrying. I've had enough. All these years wandering and gathering things, just so some other isle can pinch them. That's it. I'm settling here. Maybe one day someone will put another "Danger:

Submerged Rocks" sign on me.' And he shut his eyes and sank his toes down deep into the sea-floor silt and tried to stand as still and lifeless as any other rock of the ocean.

But he could not stop his mind from working. He could not stop himself thinking.

He thought how wrong it was that the Thurlstone was allowed to roam around wrecking other people's wigs. Then he thought sadly that the *Water Mole* was the best thing he had ever, ever found. Then he thought that, actually, Oliver and Iris were the best things he had found. He began to worry about them. He began to think that maybe the jeering weed was right to hint that he'd been cowardly. Maybe Oliver had been right. Maybe he *should* go to the Hallowed Shallows and tell the other isles what that rotten-hearted Thurlstone was up to.

'Somebody's got to do *something*!' he
said aloud. 'And Oliver and Iris are
too small, and Mr Culpeper is just an
albatross, so that somebody must be . . .
er . . . *me*!'

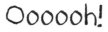

Oooooh!

said all the seaweed, tittering in that
annoying way it had. But it soon
stopped, for Cliff was on the move again,
striding and swimming as quickly as
he could towards the same horizon that
Oliver's dinghy had vanished over.

SEVEN

The sea beneath the dinghy was growing shallower. First the faces of the wading islands appeared above the waves, and then their shoulders. Oliver looked down through the clear water and saw mermaid villages clustering on the silvery sand of the sea floor. The islands set their huge stony feet down carefully, picking their way between huts and fish farms.

Iris peered down too, trying to spot people she knew. Merfolk were darting in shoals between the islands' feet, but Iris was too short-sighted to make out their faces.

Ahead, some of the isles had stopped, a crowd of great stony heads rising from the water. Their voices boomed across the sea, exchanging greetings and stories of their travels.

'Look!' said Oliver.

In the midst of the waiting isles stood the Thurlstone. There was no mistaking that towering outline, with the stolen submarine right on the top. The islands around it were all casting wary, envious looks at its fine wig.

Iris flapped the dinghy closer. A fire was blazing among the trees on the Thurlstone's top. Now and then a small, cavorting figure was silhouetted against the flames. The sound of drumming echoed across the water. There was no sign of those dangling glass globes.

Oliver felt awfully afraid. He remembered what Cliff had said about the Thurlstone's liking for blood. Was that why Stacey de Lacey had captured his parents? Perhaps he was hoping to impress the other Rambling Isles with human sacrifices!

'I have to go and find them!' he said.

The only answer was a snore from Iris. Tired out by all that tail-flapping, she had fallen asleep, draped over the dinghy's stern.

Oliver did not try to wake her. He could see that she was far too exhausted to help him free his parents. He pulled her into the dinghy and tucked a blanket from his rucksack over her. He looked around for Mr Culpeper, but the albatross had flown off to talk to some of the gulls which wheeled in white clouds around the other Rambling Isles.

Oliver scrawled a note to Iris on the inside of a caramel bar wrapper, then quickly stripped down to his special explorer's pants. He snapped on some goggles and a pair of frogman's flippers which he found in his rucksack, and dived into the sea. He struck out quickly towards the Thurlstone. Crowds of merpeople and shoals of silver fish darted beneath him, but they were all far too busy and excited to notice him. The Thurlstone's rocky head towered up into the darkening sky ahead of him. On its black sand beach only the surf

moved, but up on its top he could hear
sea monkeys cheering and squealing,
pounding on stone xylophones and
sealskin drums.

  Oliver swam and swam. He was a good
swimmer (he needed to be after all the
shark and crocodile and piranha infested
waters that Mr and Mrs Crisp had
made him swim in) but the Thurlstone
did not seem to be getting any nearer.
He realized that it was moving again,
shuffling its way right to the front of
that crowd of giants.

  A little cold finger of panic tickled
Oliver on the back of his neck. He
looked back. He had already swum a
long way. He was shivering slightly,
and although the Hallowed Shallows
might only come up to the knees of
Rambling Isles, Oliver was still far out
of his depth. He thought for a moment
of shouting for Iris, but he wasn't sure
what might happen if the Rambling

Isles or the merpeople heard him, and realized that a human being had come to their sacred seas.

Just then he noticed that the little cold finger tickling him wasn't panic; it was an actual finger, and it belonged to an actual sea monkey. He yelped

with fright as the creature doggy-
paddled round in front of him, grinning
madly. 'Eep!' it said, eyes blazing with
reflected moonbeams. It grabbed Oliver
by his wrist, and started pulling him
with it through the water, towards the
Thurlstone.

For a moment Oliver struggled, fearful
of capture. Then he looked again at the
monkey's grinning face and changed his
mind. It was trying to help him.

'Eep!' it said again, and with an
answering 'Eep!' another monkey
appeared, sliding over a wave top and
seizing Oliver by his other wrist. They
chattered at each other, kicking their

powerful little legs, hauling him forwards through the water. In ones and twos they seemed quite cute, he thought. Perhaps they weren't such bad creatures after all. Perhaps they just wanted to play?

A third monkey appeared. Then a fourth. The Thurlstone was definitely drawing nearer now. That rowdy party was still going on up above, but from nooks and crevices in the island's shores more monkeys were jumping down into the surf and swimming out to see what their friends had found. Their small hands stroked and prodded Oliver. They added their strength to his and he surged through the waves, closer and closer to the Thurlstone's beach . . .

And then, all of a sudden, there were too many monkeys. They all wanted to play with Oliver, and the newcomers began to squabble with the ones who'd found him first. Some climbed onto Oliver's head. Some wrestled his right flipper off and clung gleefully to his toes as he kicked and twisted, trying to dislodge them. He started to feel as if he was swimming in wet green fur instead of water. Monkeys were using him as a raft, scrambling up onto his shoulders and crowding on his head, forcing him under. A scrabbling, squabbling ball of monkeys surrounded him as he sank, and they were so busy taunting and fighting and teasing each other that none of them stopped to wonder if the boy in their midst could breathe under water.

Down and down they went, while
Oliver kicked and punched against the
kicking, punching monkeys. He felt his
other flipper torn off, then his goggles.

Strong little arms tugged him this way and then that, so that he was afraid they'd pull him to pieces if they didn't drown him first. At last, with a wild jerk, he jackknifed free of them and struck out blindly, leaving the monkeys to swirl and tumble behind him, not realizing yet that he'd broken out.

The Thurlstone's flank was a dim, dark wall in front of him. A deeper darkness showed in it. Oliver swam in, thinking it was a cleft that might hide him from the monkeys as he clawed his way back to the surface. In fact it was the opening of a narrow cave. Oliver remembered all those cracks and fissures he had noticed in the Thurlstone's sides when it first rose from the waves. Hollow; rotten to the core. That's what Cliff had said . . .

The passage was too narrow to turn round in, so he swam on. Heart pounding, eyes bulging, sure he was about to drown, he clawed through winding, stony passages, until at last he came up gasping for air at the centre of a flooded cavern.

Through a shaft in the ceiling moonlight

slanted, shining on the rippled water. Drums and monkey chants came down too, but softly, as if from high above. Things brushed against Oliver's legs as he trod water in the middle of the cave. Weeds? Or tentacles? He thought of the squids and octopuses that had clung to the Thurlstone's eyebrows. Was this where they lived? Panicking a bit, he swam to the side of the cave and pulled himself out onto a stony ledge. Behind him the water slopped and gurgled. He imagined disappointed monsters sinking back into the depths.

An opening in the rock wall led into another passage. This one was dry, and moonlight came down it. He crept along it. It sloped steeply upwards, round, like a stone throat. Weeds and ferns grew from the walls, and he used them as handholds while he climbed.

EIGHT

Iris woke up suddenly. 'Oliver?' she said, sitting up in the dinghy and looking around. Night had fallen while she slept. Moonlight and starlight silvered the sea. The dinghy rose and fell upon a gentle swell.

'He's gone,' said Mr Culpeper,
swooping down to land on the side of
the dinghy with a beak full of sardines.
'He left you a note.'

Iris looked around and saw the note
that Oliver had left, tucked into a gap
between the bottom boards.

'What does it say?' she wondered.

'How would I know?' said Mr
Culpeper. 'I'm an albatross.'

Iris peered at the letters with her
short-sighted eyes.

GONE TO THE THURLSTONE
BACK SOON
LOVE, OLIVER

'There you are then,'
said Mr Culpeper.

Iris looked up.
Even she could see
the Thurlstone, with

the *Water Mole* balanced on its top. 'But what about the ARMY OF MONKEYS?' she said, flapping her fins about in agitation. 'He'll be taken prisoner, just like his mum and dad!'

She launched herself over the dinghy's side and dropped with a splash into the sea. It felt good to be in the warm, scented waters of the Shallows once again, skimming over the silvery sand, flashing past the feet of Rambling Isles. But halfway to the Thurlstone she collided with a shoal of mermaids who were heading busily in the other direction.

'Ooof!' said their leader. He was a fat merman, and he was annoyed at being headbutted in the belly. 'Watch where you're going, can't you?'

'Sorry,' said Iris. 'I'm on my way to . . . '

'To the Singing Rocks, yes, yes, come on,' the merman snapped, and before she could say that, no, that wasn't where

she was going at all, Iris had been
swept up in the excitable shoal of young
mermaids. They were all done up to the
nines, with polished tails, and starfish
in their hair. Each carried her comb and
mirror. There were a few who Iris knew;
the very ones who used to laugh at her
short-sightedness.

'Where are we going?' she asked, as
they bustled her along. She hadn't been
much more than a merbaby on the last
Night of the Seawigs, and she wasn't

entirely sure what it involved.

'We're off to the Singing Rocks!' one of them said. 'To sing our songs for the Rambling Isles. Mermaids always sing on the Night of the Seawigs, remember? Come on!'

'But I can't sing!' Iris protested, trying to turn away.

They grabbed her hands and dragged her with them. 'Of course you can!' they said. 'This is no time to be modest! Come *along*!'

NINE

Up and up went Oliver, through the

maze of the bad island's empty heart.

It was not like climbing through a person's insides (that would have been horrid!). Everything seemed to be made of stone. The only thing that told Oliver he was inside a living being was that sometimes when he set his foot down or grabbed an out-jutting bit of passage wall, the whole lot *twitched*. The Thurlstone was ticklish, it seemed. Oliver tried to use only the weeds and ferns as handholds once he'd worked that out. Not all of them had deep roots. Twice he nearly fell, while leaves and clumps of rooty earth went tumbling down the shaft to spatter into the black pool where the squid and octopuses were waiting, tentacles crossed, hoping that he'd fall. But Oliver was a good climber (all the mountains and crags and lost temples he'd climbed with his mum and dad had made sure of that) and before long he was at the top.

He crawled out of a crack in the summit of the Thurlstone. The *Water Mole* and the other shipwrecks loomed over him. Monkey drums boomed, and stone xylophones clattered. The monkeys were having a wild old time, dancing round their fire, toasting sea anemones on sticks, and painting glasses and moustaches on the old stone heads. None of them noticed Oliver as he crept like a damp ghost between the trees.

Soon he reached the temple. Outside its great stone entrance was a pool, and on the pool the two glass globes that held his parents floated. Mr and Mrs Crisp were asleep, huddled in the bottoms of the globes, which clinked gently against each other from time to time, like wine glasses.

'Mum!' called Oliver softly. 'Dad!'

They did not stir. Poor things, they were just as exhausted as Iris after all their adventures.

'Mum!' he shouted, wading into the pool and banging his fists against the globes.

Still his parents did not wake, although

Dad rolled over and muttered something in his dreams. But someone had heard Oliver. A voice from behind him said,

'Ha!'

He turned round.

There stood Stacey de Lacey, with his army of monkeys around him. Some of them were still beating their drums and banging their xylophones. One held a tray of biscuits, another a cool drink for Stacey, and two others fanned him with big peacock-feather fans. The rest were just bibbling about like mad wind-up toys, full of excitement at all the mischief that lay ahead.

'You!' said Stacey de Lacey, pointing rudely at Oliver. 'So here you are, come to thieve and sneak and spoil my plans!'

'I just want my mum and dad back!' Oliver promised.

'Well you can't have them!' jeered Stacey. 'The Thurlstone needs them. They are the finishing touches on his wig. They could make all the difference. They're just the sort of thing that will make him stand out.'

'But why do you care so much about the Thurlstone winning?' Oliver asked miserably.

'Ah!' said Stacey de Lacey. 'We've got a deal, me and the Thurlstone. If I help him win this seawig thing, then he'll help me. Imagine the power I'll have, with this great big giant at my command! And other Rambling Isles will follow the Thurlstone, when they see his wonderful wig! The winner of Seawigs Night is a sort of king; they'll have to do as he says. We'll stomp New York, smash London, sit on Shanghai. The whole world will tremble before us! Nobody will *dare* say I've got a girly name then!'

'But you *have* got a girly name,' grumbled Oliver.

'MONKEYS!' howled Stacey de Lacey.

Oliver tried to fend the monkeys off, but soon he was pinned down under a gibbering heap of them. Meanwhile, some others had gone rushing into a side chamber of the temple and reappeared bowling a third glass globe. Some held it steady while the rest unscrewed its lid. Then Oliver was monkeyhandled into it, and the lid screwed shut behind him.

Stacey de Lacey grinned in at him, his leering face stretched out of shape by the thick glass. 'Now the Thurlstone's wig is finished!' he chortled. 'Not just *two* stupid Crisps, but the whole set!'

Tittering with mischief, the monkeys rolled Oliver away. Mr and Mrs Crisp had been woken by the noise and were sitting up inside their globes, watching sadly as their son was trundled past them.

'I'm sorry!' mouthed Oliver, through the glass.

A reef of dark rocks rose from the Hallowed Shallows, with the waves breaking whitely around it. Wet stone shone in the moonlight. The mermaids scrambled through the surf and up onto the reef's rocky ledges. There they sat, each with her comb and her mirror and her long hair blown sideways on the breeze. Their plump choirmaster bobbed like a seal in the waves and clapped his hands to get the mermaids' attention. 'Just time for a quick practice, girls! Sing up!'

So they sang, and their voices blended with the voices of the sea and wind. All over the Hallowed Shallows the Rambling Isles forgot their nervousness and listened. Up on the Thurlstone's head Oliver and his mum and dad heard that song, and it sent shivers riffling down their spines. (They couldn't listen for long, though: they were busy being rolled across the Thurlstone's summit by those monkeys, and dangled over its edge.)

'Stop, stop, stop!' the fat merman shouted, clapping his hands over his

ears. The song of
mermaids was meant
to sound strange and
unearthly, but not *this*
strange and unearthly.
'Someone's singing
flat!' he said
accusingly, glaring at
the rows of singers.

Iris knew it was her.
She blushed deep red.
The merman spotted
her and pointed. 'You!
Sing for me!'

Iris drew a deep
breath and sang as
loudly and sweetly as
she could. An awful,

strangled note emerged, so piercing that the nearest mermaids' mirrors cracked.

'Stop! Stop!' the merman shouted. 'What a disgraceful racket! What were you thinking of, joining our choir with a voice like that! Be off with you!'

Iris started to explain that she hadn't meant to join the choir at all, then decided that there wasn't time and splashed back into the sea. She couldn't imagine why she'd wanted to find her way home to all these silly merpeople. Her new friends were much more fun. All she cared about now was rescuing Oliver.

TEN

The Hallowed Shallows were crowded
with Rambling Isles now; hundreds of
them, some large, some small. They
seemed to be waiting for something.
Oliver waited too, dangling from the
Thurlstone's brow, his glass globe
swinging to and fro in its creaking basket
of ropes. When would the judging begin?

147

Stacey de Lacey was running about busily on the Thurlstone's head, shouting orders at his monkeys while they did a bit of last-minute polishing and tidied scraps of seawig that had been blown skew-whiff by the wind.

At last, on the far horizon, a tiny speck appeared, drawing quickly closer. The islands all mumbled and muttered to each other, turning to look. Soon, Oliver could see that the approaching thing was another Rambling Isle, striding purposefully through the waves. On either side of it the wave crests foamed, and the foam took on the form of galloping horses. It was the Chief Island, who had won the last Night of

the Seawigs. The white horses of the
sea formed an honour guard for her,
and the mermaids on the Singing Rocks
started to sing again, properly now
that they didn't have Iris helping. The
Chief Island (her name was Dambulay)
waded into the Shallows and stopped.
On her summit towered a massive wig
of trees and flowers and grasses, with
rainbows knotted in it, and the prows of
Viking longships jutting out like ornate
hairpins. She looked at her fellow islands
with pride and sadness, and then quickly
shook her head, so that the old wig came
apart, the rainbows drifting away, the
rotten timbers of the old ships tumbling
down her sides into the sea.

   'Ahhh!' said the Rambling Isles, and
'Oooh!' Even the Thurlstone made a
               deep rumbling sound, out
                        of respect for

Dambulay's wonderful wig.

'Never mind,' said Dambulay sadly. 'It was a good wig, but it was old, and now I can start again, and collect a whole new one. But first we must see who here has the finest seawig. Which of us has found the prettiest things on their wanderings? Who shall be the winner tonight, and Chief Island for the next seven years?'

The islands shifted a little. The ones whose wigs were really poor, or had suffered in the wind, slunk backwards into deeper water. Some eyed up the drifting bits of Dambulay's wig that still bobbed upon the waves, wondering if they could make some last-minute changes without the others noticing. The prouder ones preened themselves, hoping to attract the votes of their neighbours. The island with the wig of drizzled sand drew many admiring looks. So did another, which had a crown of whalebones. But none could compare with the splendour of the Thurlstone, with its shipwrecks and those three glass globes, from which three captive humans gawped. One by one the islands turned until they were all gazing at it.

Oliver, trapped in his hanging globe, pounded his hands against the inside of the glass and shouted, 'No! It's not fair! The Thurlstone cheated!' But the mermaids were singing still, and their voices drowned out his protests. His parents waved and shouted too, but the Rambling Isles thought they were only pleading for their freedom. Captive humans! How original! No island had worn captive humans for *centuries*!

'Thurlstone!' said one of the isles, in a deep, rumbly voice.

'Thurlstone!' said another, softer.

'Thurlstone!' cried a third, in a voice like the boom of surf in deserted coves.

Iris popped up beside the Thurlstone's left knee, red-faced and breathless after her hasty swim from the reef. She pointed up at the isle and shouted, but there was no way she could make herself heard over the voices of the Rambling Isles.

'Thurlstone! Thurlstone! Thurlstone!' Even the one with the wig of whalebones, who had been hoping to win, saw which way the tide was running and added his voice to those of the others 'Thurlstone! Let Thurlstone be the winner.'

Just then the song of the mermaids rose in a wild crescendo, and suddenly Iris saw how she might be able to save Oliver and his family, even if all else was lost. She took a deep breath, and sang the same note she had sung for the merman choirmaster a few moments before. She sang louder this time; as loud and as shrill as she could. She sang till her face turned purple. Before, her voice had been enough to break the mermaids' mirrors.

This time it made the Rambling Isles clap their hands over their ears, and put the other mermaids off their song.

Oliver, swinging in his globe, saw a fine frost of cracks start to spread across the glass.

Tisssh! Crasssh! Smassh! The three globes shattered. Icefalls of glass cascaded down the Thurlstone's cliffs. Into the sea dropped Mr and Mrs Crisp.

But what of Oliver? Iris peered about, trying not to be distracted by the hoots of the angry islands, who were all outraged that a mere mermaid had dared to interrupt that solemn moment.

Ah, there he was! Clinging to a root which jutted from the Thurlstone's rocky forehead. But just as Iris saw him a great smother of foam came down on her. The Thurlstone turned towards her, swirling the skirts of the sea.

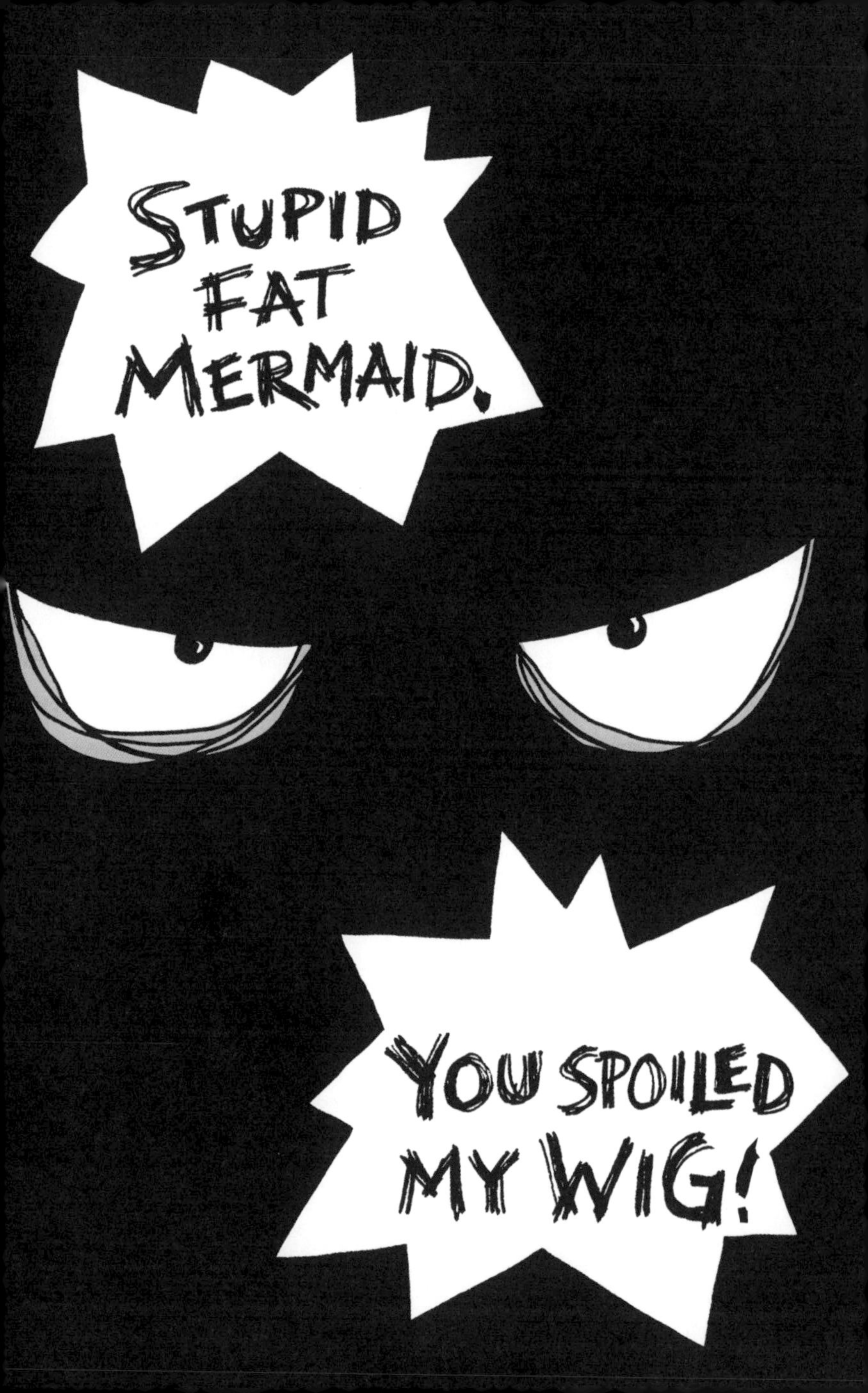
STUPID FAT MERMAID.
YOU SPOILED MY WIG!

Iris darted out of the way as the Thurlstone's huge foot tried to squash her. She plunged down under it, almost to the silver sand of the sea floor, and then rose up on the other side. As she broke the surface there Mr Culpeper came flapping over her, squawking, 'Here they are!' She saw Mr and Mrs Crisp, clinging together, tossed up and down like two corks on the waves which the angry island was creating. She seized each of them by a hand and swam with them to calmer water.

But Oliver knew nothing about any of this.

Clutching at roots and rocky pimples, he had heaved himself back up the Thurlstone's steep face. There he saw sea monkeys running in every direction, while furious Stacey de Lacey kicked them about like furry green footballs.

'It's all gone wrong!' Stacey raged. 'We'll be disqualified! Unless . . . '

'Gaaargh!' roared the Thurlstone. Other islands blundered away from it, scared of its rage and the way it lashed its clumsy stone fists about like massive hammers. Stacey de Lacey scrambled onto his viewing platform on the island's brow and grabbed his loudhailer. 'The Thurlstone is still the winner!' he bellowed. 'You chose him, and he won, fair and square! And now you'd better do what he says, or my monkeys will come and mess your wigs up!'

Sea monkeys spilled down the Thurlstone's face like a river of snot. They spread across the ocean, gibbering with wild glee as the waves lifted them up and down. But above the shouting of Stacey de Lacey and the roars of the Thurlstone, the hoots of frightened isles and the squeals of the monkeys, a new voice boomed out.

'STOP!' it said.

The Rambling Isles looked round. The monkeys too. Even the Thurlstone stopped roaring and glanced over its huge stone shoulder.

Another Rambling Isle had arrived. A small and shabby isle, with nothing on its head but the sad remnants of a not-very-good wig, and a confused narwhal which it had just scooped up. At the sight of him, Iris jumped clean out of the water and turned a cartwheel above the Crisps' bewildered heads.

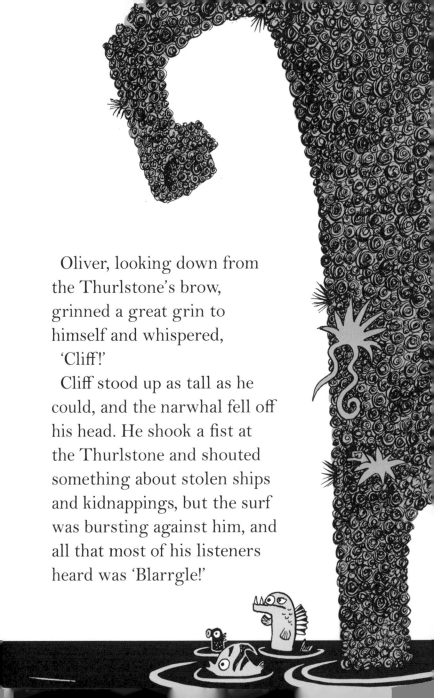

Oliver, looking down from
the Thurlstone's brow,
grinned a great grin to
himself and whispered,
  'Cliff!'
Cliff stood up as tall as he
could, and the narwhal fell off
his head. He shook a fist at
the Thurlstone and shouted
something about stolen ships
and kidnappings, but the surf
was bursting against him, and
all that most of his listeners
heard was 'Blarrgle!'

Oliver, from his high vantage point, could see that the poor island's knees were knocking together, but still Cliff stood his ground as the Thurlstone, with seabed-shaking stomps, strode angrily towards him.

Poor Cliff! All the way from the Sarcastic Sea he had kept telling himself that his fellow Rambling Isles would help him to teach the Thurlstone a lesson. Now he could see that they were all as scared of it as he was. As they edged nervously away he realized that he was going to have to face it alone.

Which was very bad, because the Thurlstone was bigger and stronger and fiercer than Cliff, and up on its head Stacey de Lacey was yelling, 'Smash him, Thurlstone! Bash him up! Stamp him down!'

'Leave him alone!' shouted Oliver, jumping up from his hiding place. A monkey drum rolled past him as the

Thurlstone lurched towards Cliff, and Oliver snatched it and flung it at Stacey de Lacey. It missed, but it made Stacey look round, and he forgot about Cliff and charged angrily at Oliver instead.

Oliver ran away from him, zigzagging between the trees, looking for something he could use to defend himself. Near the pool by the temple he found one of the peacock-feather fans lying where a careless monkey had dropped it. It looked a flimsy, feather-dustery sort of thing, but he picked it up anyway.

That was when the idea came to him.

He could hear Stacey de Lacey panting through the trees behind him, spluttering threats and curses. The ground beneath him shivered as the Thurlstone let out another cry of rage. Oliver ran between the trees to where one of those fissures opened; the cracks which led down into the island's hollow insides. He took a deep breath, and jumped in. *Dump—bump—crash* he went, bruising himself as he tumbled down through stony tubes and crannies. He snatched at out-juttings of rock to slow himself, and the Thurlstone flinched just as it had before. How could something so big and stony-seeming be so ticklish? Oliver wondered. And what would happen when he really started tickling?

He found a foothold, raised his feather fan, and set to work.

The Thurlstone swung a huge fist at Cliff. Cliff ducked, and the blow missed by a whisker. The Thurlstone growled and rumbled, readying itself to strike again.

But suddenly it stopped. Something was *moving* inside it. Something that *tickled* . . . It writhed. A shipwreck dropped off its wig and splashed into the sea. *'Arrrararaggaharauaaraga!'* said the Thurlstone (or something along those lines). Another ship fell—the *Water Mole* this time. It landed near the spot where Mr and Mrs Crisp were treading water, and Iris hustled them aboard it.

'Stoppit!' howled the Thurlstone, but Oliver wouldn't stop. Deep in the bad old isle's insides he tickled and he tickled, mercilessly jabbing his feather fan into all the cracks and fissures he could reach, wriggling and jiggling it there.

The Thurlstone clutched its sides and howled. It stumbled and staggered, throwing up sheets of spray, making waves which slapped against the faces of the other Rambling Isles and rocked the *Water Mole* and her passengers wildly up and down. A stone head tumbled off the Thurlstone's summit. A few last sea monkeys jumped off the cliffs like rats abandoning a sinking ship, cannonballing into the water. The ancient temple quivered, cracked, crumbled. Bits and pieces of it cascaded past the Thurlstone's face to smash into the water. Other bits of his wig came loose too; wreaths of seaweed, boulders, trees . . .

'You vandal!' Stacey de Lacey screamed, dodging a toppling stone head and shouting down the crack that Oliver had vanished into. 'You spoilsport! You're ruining everything!'

Down beneath his feet, Oliver just went

on tickling and tickling . . .

Until, with a creak, a black crack opened, splitting the Thurlstone's summit in two.

Other, smaller cracks spread out from it. Stacey de Lacey watched in horror as they surrounded him. More creaks and groans and straining sounds filled the air. The Thurlstone had quaked and quivered and shuddered and shaken so much that it was coming completely to pieces. Down on the water, Iris and the Crisps watched cracks cover the Thurlstone's stupid, startled face like a

black net. Then, in a slither of shards
and a cloud of dust and upflung spray,
the Rambling Isle exploded.

  For a moment they saw Stacey de Lacey,
clinging to the top of one great fragment,
yelling as it toppled. For a moment
they thought they saw Oliver, tumbling
free with a big feather fan flapping like
a wing above him. Then the spray hid
everything.

Oliver hit the water hard as the Thurlstone came apart around him. He plunged deep enough to brush his fingers over the silver sand beneath, and came up gasping for air. He trod water and looked around, while the upflung spray fell upon the waves like rain.

There was no Thurlstone any more, only a few scattered chunks, small islets whose heads barely poked above the waters even here in the Shallows. One by one they opened little black beady eyes of their own and blinked. They were brand new Rambling Isles, bashful in the presence of so many bigger ones.

Oliver laughed, swimming between them, till there ahead of him he saw the *Water Mole*, still just about afloat, with his mum and dad and Iris and Mr Culpeper all waving at him from its upper deck.

Iris pulled him aboard, and he ran and hugged Mum, then Dad. The ancient submarine was sinking fast, but Cliff waded over and supported it before it could settle to the sea floor. 'Wow! That was really amazing!' said a strand of Sarcastic Seaweed, hanging down in front of Cliff's face, and it sounded as if it really meant it.

The other islands shuffled closer, trying to look as if they had been right at Cliff's side all along and not a bit scared of the Thurlstone. Some mumbled that Cliff had done well; others explained that they had never trusted the Thurlstone. A few of the quicker-thinking ones scooped up bits of the Thurlstone's scattered wig and added them to their own, because it was pretty clear that a new winner would have to be chosen.

It was Dambulay who was the first
to say, 'Thank you.' She looked at Iris
and Oliver, then at Cliff. 'Thank you.
You have saved us from awarding
the greatest honour of our kind to a
bad creature who did not deserve it.
You have been brave, while we were
cowardly. What is your name?'

'Cliff,' said Cliff, blushing a bit. 'This
is my seawig,' he added, scooping up
the *Water Mole* and setting it on his top
again. 'The Thurlstone stole it from me.
There were some other bits too, but they
got lost.'

The Rambling Isles all looked at him.
The *Water Mole* did not look nearly as
splendid on top of Cliff as it had when
the Thurlstone wore it. The strands
of weed which he had carried with him
from the Sarcastic Sea did their best
to look decorative, and Mr Culpeper
perched on the *Water Mole*'s bow with
his wings outspread, but it still looked

a bit shabby and scruffy. Even so, Dambulay turned to the other islands and said, 'I think it is clear what we must do. Cliff is the bravest of us, and his seawig is certainly the most . . . interesting. He is the winner of this Night of the Seawigs.'

'Yay!' shouted Iris and Oliver and Mr Culpeper. Mr and Mrs Crisp clapped politely—they were a bit confused, but they were starting to get the hang of things. Even the weed looked pleased.

But Cliff slowly shook his head.

'Not me,' he said. 'I can't hang around here in the Shallows, being feted and fussed over. I don't care about this Seawig competition any more. Let Thrumcap be the winner, or Dimsey. I have to take my friends home.'

Then, with all the other Rambling Isles looking on, he turned and waded away. Up on his head Mr and Mrs Crisp fetched out their cameras and took

photo after photo of the watching
isles and the mermaids. But, either
because of some magic of the
Shallows, or because the cameras
had been battered too badly
during their adventures, not one
of those pictures ever came out.

As for Oliver, he just clung to the *Water Mole*'s barnacled rail and stared, trying to take it all in. He saw the unearthly purplish sky and the pale sea, the white horses galloping in the wave crests, the mermaids playing in Cliff's wake like dolphins. He saw the Rambling Isles in all their finery. He did his best to fix it in his mind for ever, and unlike the photographs, his memories *did* come out. He kept them always, and they never faded.

Not far away, a fragment of the roof from the Thurlstone's temple floated on the waves. Stacey de Lacey sat on it, bedraggled and alone, using another, smaller piece of flotsam for a paddle. He was paddling himself away from the Hallowed Shallows as quickly as he could. He was hoping that, if the sea stayed calm and the wind in the right direction, he might paddle all the way home. He wondered if his parents would have noticed that he'd been away.

'Eep?' said a little voice. Webbed paws appeared over the edge of his raft. A sea monkey pulled itself aboard and snuggled down against Stacey's left knee. He patted its head, feeling rather glad that he still had a friend left.

'Eep!' said another monkey, scrambling out of the sea behind him.

'Eep! Eep! Eeber! Eeeple!' said a dozen more.

'No!' cried
Stacey. 'Back in
the sea with you! There
isn't room!'
But there's no arguing with sea
monkeys, and the sea around his raft was

green with them. They
swarmed aboard. When there
wasn't a single inch of bare wood left
without a little wet green body sitting
on it they started sitting on Stacey
de Lacey instead, and when there
wasn't a single inch of *him* without a
monkey on they took to sitting on top of
each other, until a teetering, bickering
mound of monkeys was piled high on
the wallowing raft, with Stacey de
Lacey in the middle of it somewhere,
still glumly paddling.

ELEVEN

Mr and Mrs Crisp were very meek
during the journey home. They knew
that their terrible adventures had all
happened because they'd been so eager
to explore the islands, and they knew of
the dangers that Oliver had braved to
rescue them. 'No more exploring for us,'
they agreed, sitting with Oliver, Iris, and
Mr Culpeper beside the camp fire that
they had lit on Cliff's head.

But Oliver knew they didn't mean it. After all the thrilling new things they'd seen, they would soon be itching to go exploring again. They wouldn't even have to worry about money any more, because the old trunks which they'd dragged out of the *Water Mole* to use as seats around the fire turned out to be stuffed full of Spanish gold. For the moment, though, they seemed very happy to be safe and back with Oliver again. And they were happier still a few days later, when Cliff waded into Deepwater Bay, and they saw their house and the dear old explorermobile standing where they had left them.

Oliver wasn't happy though. He was glad to see dry land again, but he didn't feel that surge of joy he'd felt when Mum drove them down the lane to the house that first day. He still wanted a home just as badly, but he wanted something else now, too: he wanted to be with Cliff, and Iris. He was going to miss them. He would even miss crotchety Mr Culpeper.

So he stood quietly watching while the shore came closer, and his mum and dad did a happy-to-be-home dance on Cliff's golden sand. And when they said, 'Look, Ollie, it's our house!' and 'Aren't you glad to be back?' he nodded and said that he was. But Mr and Mrs Crisp could tell he wasn't, and they looked solemnly at one another. They both knew how sweet and sad it can be to want two different things so completely.

'Don't worry,' said Mr Crisp, putting an arm round Oliver's shoulders. 'We'll find a way.'

Mrs Crisp knelt down and tapped politely on Cliff's forehead. 'We were wondering,' she said, 'if you've nowhere else to go, perhaps you'd like to stay here in Deepwater Bay? It looks so much nicer with an island in it.'

So Cliff found a comfortable spot for himself just offshore, and that night the Crisp family slept in actual beds, inside a proper house, for the first time in years. (Iris made up a bed for herself in the bath.) Early the next morning Oliver took the dinghy up the coast to Farsight Cove with Iris swimming alongside.

The beach optician was in his usual spot on the sand, and he looked very startled when Iris came out of the sea. He had never really believed in mermaids either, and his beach optician's stall was just an excuse to get away from his noisy family and spend a few hours each day sitting quietly by the sea. But he hid his surprise as best as he could, and tested Iris's eyes, and presented her with a very fetching pair of spectacles. 'Wow!' she said, gazing about her at the cliffs, the sand, the sea. Suddenly everything looked very sharp and clear. She wasn't sure she liked it, though she supposed she would get used to it in time. 'So *that's* what you look like!' she said, peering at Oliver through the thick lenses. 'Oh.'

'What do you mean, "Oh"?' asked Oliver.

'Nothing,' said Iris.

Meanwhile, Mr Crisp had been drawing plans on the backs of old envelopes, and Mrs Crisp had been telephoning local builders and asking if they would accept payment in ancient Spanish doubloons. It turned out that they would, and soon the Crisp's old house had been dismantled, and rebuilt on top of Cliff. ('It's the best wig a Rambling Isle ever had!' he said delightedly, when it was finished.) Of course that meant that there was no longer room for the *Water Mole*, but the old submarine wasn't really suited to being out in the open air anyway, and its timbers were beginning to crumble as they dried out. So they carefully lowered it to the bottom of Deepwater Bay, and Iris set up house inside it. When Oliver came home from school in the afternoons, he'd often dive down to visit her, holding his breath for as long as he could to see her latest improvements. Now that she could see clearly, Iris had grown rather house-proud, and she had gathered odds and ends from the seabed to decorate her new home. Oliver thought the old toilet bowl she had on display in the centre of her kitchen table looked rather odd, but she'd arranged such a colourful collection of live sea anemones in it that he had to confess it brightened up the place. She'd also hung up several mirrors, which Oliver noticed were all cracked, but he was too polite to ask if she'd been singing. The more she showed him, the faster he'd nod and approve it all, as his cheeks went redder and redder from lack of air. But Iris was always pleased to see him making the effort.

Even Mr Culpeper stayed. He
complained that the island was getting
very built up, and he enjoyed telling
other visiting birds that *he* could
remember when it was all just rocks
and grass, but he built himself a large,
raggedy nest on the roof just above
Oliver's bedroom, and enjoyed waking
Oliver up each morning by leaning
down and shouting 'Time for school!'
through the window. Oliver didn't mind
though: he *enjoyed* school.

Mr and Mrs Crisp have made a little bridge to link Cliff to the mainland, wide enough for the explorermobile or the cars of visiting friends to drive across. But it isn't a permanent bridge: it can be folded back onto Cliff's shores whenever the Crisps want to remember that they really do live on an island. And sometimes, in Oliver's school holidays, or on other days when they just feel like it, they say to Cliff, 'This feels like an exploring day.' Then they fold the bridge away, and Cliff wades off in search of strange seas and forgotten coves, with Mr and Mrs Crisp safe and snug in their own living room, Mr Culpeper keeping watch from his nest, and Iris and Oliver riding on the beach.

It is by far the most comfortable way to go exploring.

ABOUT THE AUTHORS

PHILIP REEVE

TRAVELLED FAR AND WIDE TO INTERVIEW THE ISLANDS ON WHOSE STORIES THIS BOOK IS BASED. HE HAS ADOPTED ONE OF THE THURLSTONE SCATTERLINGS AND KEEPS IT IN HIS POND AT HOME, WHERE, ON QUIET AFTERNOONS, IT MAY BE HEARD HUMMING SEA SHANTIES. HE IS ALSO THE AUTHOR OF MORTAL ENGINES, HERE LIES ARTHUR, FEVER CRUMB, GOBLINS, AND MANY MORE BOOKS.

NO FISH WERE HARMED IN THE MAKING OF THIS BOOK (EXCEPT FOR GERALD, WHO NEVER PAID ATTENTION AND PROBABLY DESERVED IT).

SARAH McINTYRE

SPENDS HALF OF EACH YEAR ADRIFT IN THE INDIAN OCEAN ON A RAFT WHICH SHE HAS BUILT FROM ICE CREAM TUBS. A STEADY STREAM OF MERMAIDS VISIT HER THERE TO HAVE THEIR PORTRAITS PAINTED. HER FAVOURITE PART OF THE JOB WAS EATING ALL THE ICE CREAM.

IN HER SPARE TIME, SHE HAS ILLUSTRATED MANY BOOKS AND COMICS, INCLUDING VERN AND LETTUCE, WHEN TITUS TOOK THE TRAIN, YOU CAN'T SCARE A PRINCESS!, AND MORRIS THE MANKIEST MONSTER.

Iris's hair styled by Chez Mollusque

FABULOUS! NOW READ THAT BIT BACK TO ME...

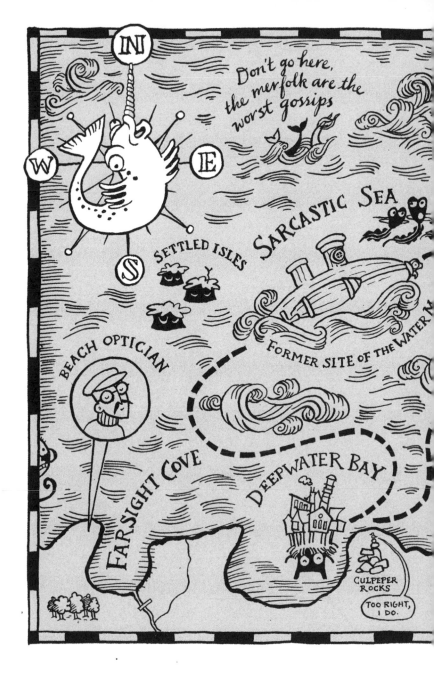

SLIGHTLY UNSETTLED ISLE

THE HALLOWED SHALLOWS

More gossipy
merfolk here
(grumpy, too)

Best mermaid fishing grounds

certain moody seagull ALBATROSS
likes to hang
round here

ROCKS

NOVAE SEAWIGGUS
AS EXPLORED BY THE CRISPS
with expert advice from Iris

AND COLIN

COLIN THE CRAB HAS HAD SMALL PARTS IN MANY BEST-SELLING BOOKS. THIS IS THE FIRST TIME HE HAS MANAGED TO GET INTO EVERY PICTURE ... OR AT LEAST, ALL THE IMPORTANT PICTURES. HE WOULD LIKE TO THANK HIS AGENT, HIS MUM AND DAD, HIS AUNTIE JOY, HIS 37,000 BROTHERS AND SISTERS, EV... WHO...